Baby Dragon

Amy Ehrlich   *illustrated by* Will Hillenbrand

WALKER BOOKS
AND SUBSIDIARIES
LONDON · BOSTON · SYDNEY · AUCKLAND

One afternoon, Baby Dragon's mother said,
"Grandma isn't feeling well. I must go to see her."
She warmed Baby Dragon's face and tickled his tail.
"Wait for me by this red fern," she said. "I'll be back
by morning."

Baby Dragon waited.

He drew a picture in the earth.

He counted his claws.

He took a nap.

Then Frog hopped by.

"What are you doing?" Frog asked.

"I'm waiting for my mother," said Baby Dragon.

"Don't wait," said Frog. "Come and play with me."

"No," said Baby Dragon. "If I come with you,
 my mother won't be able to find me."

"Goodbye then," said Frog. And he hopped away.

Baby Dragon looked all around.
He couldn't see his mother anywhere.

He nibbled some grass.

He caught a mosquito.

He took a nap.

Then Weasel crept by.

"What are you doing?" Weasel asked.

"I'm waiting for my mother," said Baby Dragon.

"Don't wait," said Weasel. "I know where we can find ripe bananas to eat. I'll take you there."

"No," said Baby Dragon. "If I come with you, my mother won't be able to find me."

"Goodbye then," said Weasel. And she crept away.

Baby Dragon sang himself a song:
"I want my mother.
I want her here –
to warm her face
and curl up near!"

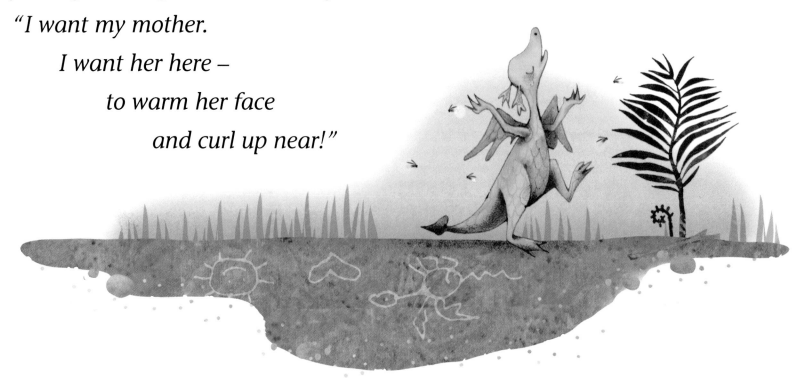

Baby Dragon looked all around,
but he still couldn't see his mother.
She had said she'd be back by morning.
Would morning ever come?

As Baby Dragon thought about his mother, he got sadder and sadder. He was too sad even to take a nap.

Then Crocodile glided by.

"What are you doing?" Crocodile asked.

"I'm waiting for my mother," said Baby Dragon.

"Jump on my back," said Crocodile. "I'll take you to find her."

Baby Dragon looked all around.

The sun was setting. The trees were black against the sky. But he still couldn't see his mother.

Crocodile was waiting.

Baby Dragon closed his eyes tightly and jumped onto Crocodile's back.

Night birds called as they glided up the river.
Crocodile swam for a long time with Baby Dragon
on his back.
Baby Dragon looked at the shore.
He could see rocks and turtles and water buffaloes,
but he couldn't see his mother.

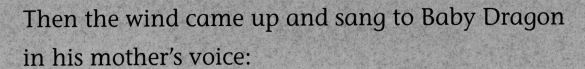

Then the wind came up and sang to Baby Dragon
in his mother's voice:

"Wait here. I'll be back.

I'll be back by morning."

"STOP!" said Baby Dragon to Crocodile.

"I want to go back and wait for my mother."

But Crocodile only laughed.

"Oh, no," he said. "I'm taking you to my swamp
up the river. I'm going to feed you to my children."

Baby Dragon knew he would have to be brave.

He waited until Crocodile swam past a log.

Then he closed his eyes tightly
and JUMPED!

The log slipped. Baby Dragon
almost fell into the water.

But he held on tightly and paddled the log to the shore.
Crocodile kept on swimming. He didn't realize that
Baby Dragon had gone.

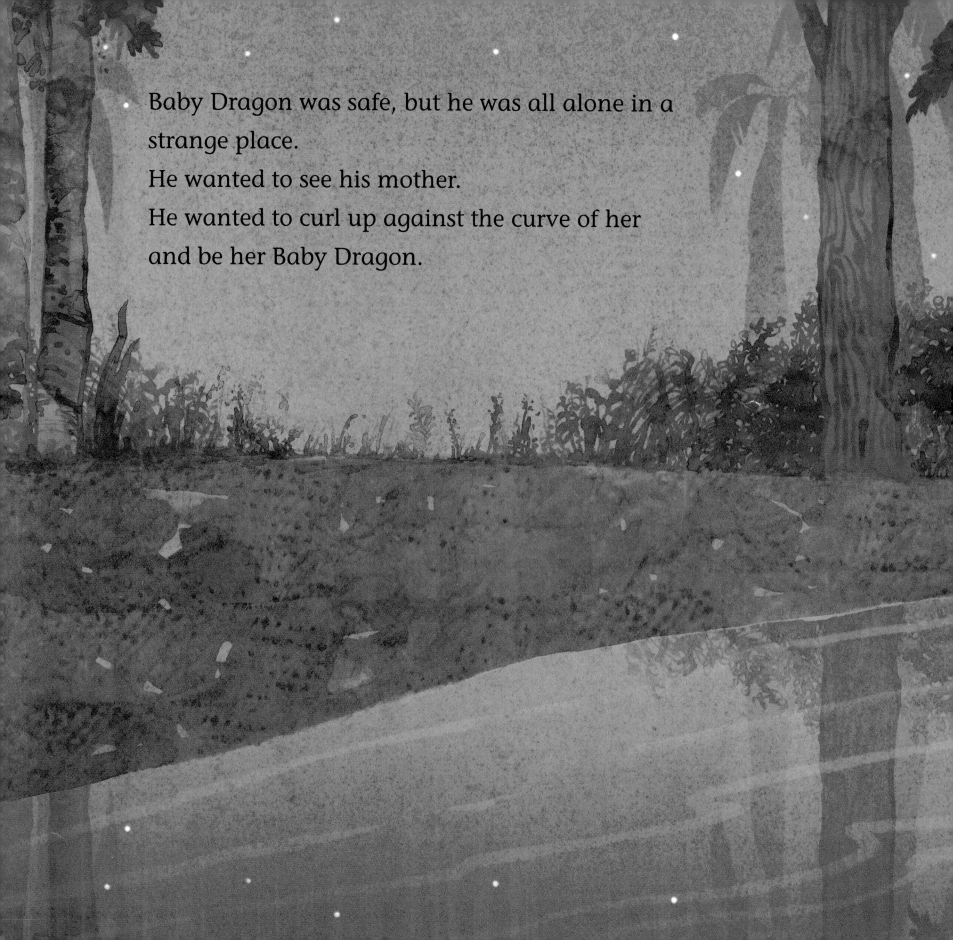

Baby Dragon was safe, but he was all alone in a strange place.

He wanted to see his mother.

He wanted to curl up against the curve of her and be her Baby Dragon.

She had told him to wait by the red fern, but he hadn't waited.

She had said she'd be back by morning, but morning hadn't come...

Morning hadn't come!
Maybe there was still time.
Maybe if he went back to the red fern,
his mother would still be able to find him.

The stars were out. The moon shone.
Baby Dragon turned and walked back along
the river, following the path of moonlight.

It was a long way, but Baby Dragon
put one foot in front of the other,

one foot in front of the other,

one foot in front of the other, until he
came to the red fern where his mother
had left him.

It was still dark.

Baby Dragon waited for morning.

He heard storks splashing in the water.

He felt the wind die down.

He watched the sky grow light.

And then his mother came.

She was very glad to see him.

Baby Dragon curled against the curve of her and

they told each other about their adventures.

"I've missed you so much," said Baby Dragon.

"But I said I'd be back by morning," said his mother.

"And look – morning is here."

"Will you always come back?" asked Baby Dragon.

"Of course I will," she said.

Baby Dragon warmed his mother's face with

his baby dragon breath.

Then he ran to find Frog. It was time to play!

For Jackson, Quinn and Jacob
A. E.

*To my friend Tom Erndt. Thank you
for drawing your dragon for me!*
W. H.

First published 2008 by Walker Books Ltd
87 Vauxhall Walk, London SE11 5HJ

2 4 6 8 10 9 7 5 3 1

Text © 2008 Amy Ehrlich
Illustrations © 2008 Will Hillenbrand

The right of Amy Ehrlich and Will Hillenbrand to be identified as author and illustrator
respectively of this work has been asserted by them in accordance with
the Copyright, Designs and Patents Act 1988.

This book has been typeset in Stone Informal.

Printed in Singapore.

British Library Cataloguing in Publication Data:
a catalogue record for this book is available from the British Library

ISBN 978-1-4063-1236-2

www.walkerbooks.co.uk